IF KIDS COULD DRIVE

WRITTEN BY
MARISA KOLLMEIER
AND TEEPOO RIAZ

ILLUSTRATED BY
BRANDON DORMAN

JIMMY Patterson Books
Little, Brown and Company
New York Boston London

Wouldn't it be great if kids could drive?

There would be bubble-gum roads
and roller-coaster highways to take you
wherever you wanted to go.

If kids could drive . . . your car would be powered by milkshakes
(and you would be too!).

All the roadside restaurants would serve only your favorite foods!

There would always be a jungle gym nearby where you could stretch your legs.

And every single trip
would include a stop at Adventure Land!

If kids could drive . . . you would make the rules of the road!

Which is why cars would need marshmallow bumpers.

Your car would definitely fly!

If kids could drive . . . you'd have to keep your eyes on the road—
because you'd never know who (or what) might be crossing it.

If kids could drive . . . all trucks would have super-special deliveries—just for you!

If kids could drive . . . when the weather took a turn, you could snuggle in for a nap.

If kids could drive . . . parents would ALWAYS sit in the back!

And getting there together would be the best part of every trip.

FOR INDIA AND GEMMA,
WHOSE IMAGINATIONS CREATED THIS STORY AND DRIVE OUR DREAMS — M. K. AND T. R.

FOR MY DAD, WHOSE DRIVING IS ALWAYS FUN, HAIR-RAISING,
ADVENTUROUS, AND COLORFUL — B. D.

Text copyright © 2021 by Marisa Kollmeier and Teepoo Riaz
Illustrations copyright © 2021 by Brandon Dorman

JIMMY Patterson Books / Little, Brown and Company
Hachette Book Group
1290 Avenue of the Americas, New York, NY 10104
JamesPatterson.org

First Edition: May 2021

JIMMY Patterson Books is an imprint of Little, Brown and Company, a division of Hachette Book Group, Inc. The Little, Brown name and logo are trademarks of Hachette Book Group, Inc. The JIMMY Patterson Books® name and logo are trademarks of JBP Business, LLC.

The publisher is not responsible for websites (or their content) that are not owned by the publisher.

The Hachette Speakers Bureau provides a wide range of authors for speaking events. To find out more, go to hachettespeakersbureau.com or call (866) 376-6591.

Library of Congress Cataloging-in-Publication Data

Names: Kollmeier, Marisa, author. | Riaz, Teepoo, author. | Dorman, Brandon, illustrator. Title: If kids could drive / Marisa Kollmeier and Teepoo Riaz ; illustrated by Brandon Dorman. Description: First edition. | New York : Little, Brown and Company, [2021] | "JIMMY Patterson Books." | Audience: Ages 3–6. Audience: Grades K–1. | Summary: Imagines a world in which children would drive cars with marshmallow bumpers to roadside restaurants with only children's menus, and every trip would include a stop at an amusement park. Identifiers: LCCN 2019047785 (print) | LCCN 2019047786 (ebook) ISBN 9780316494090 (hardcover) | ISBN 9780316494113 (ebook) Subjects: CYAC: Automobile driving—Fiction. | Imagination—Fiction. Classification: LCC PZ7.1.K67564 2021 (print) | LCC PZ7.1.K67564 2021 (ebook) | DDC [E]—dc23 LC record available at https://lccn.loc.gov/2019047785 LC ebook record available at https://lccn.loc.gov/2019047786

10 9 8 7 6 5 4 3 2 1

Printed in China

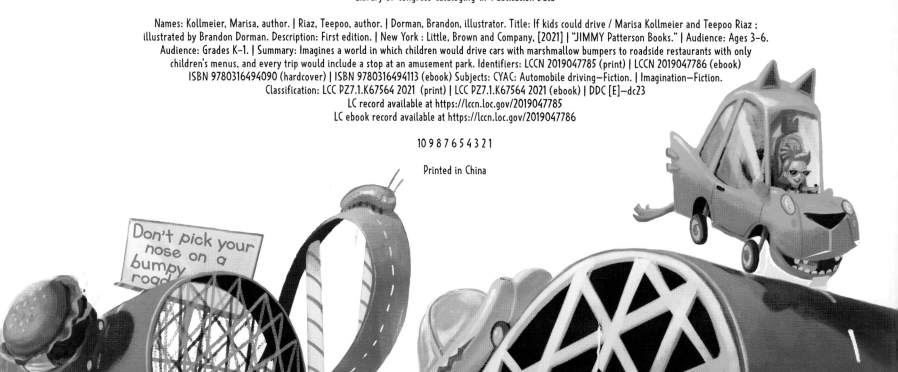